DATE DUE

FOLLETT

To Laura

Henry Holt and Company, LLC

Publishers since 1866

115 West 18th Street

New York, New York 10011

Henry Holt is a registered trademark of Henry Holt and Company, LLC

Distributed in Canada by H. B. Fenn and Company Ltd.

Library of Congress Cataloging-in-Publication Data

McCarty, Peter.

Hondo and Fabian / Peter McCarty.

Summary: Hondo the dog gets to go to the beach and play with his
friend Fred, while Fabian the cat spends the day at home.

1. Dogs—Juvenile fiction. 2. Cats—Juvenile fiction.

[1. Dogs—Fiction. 2. Cats—Fiction. 3. Pets—Fiction.] I. Title.

PZ10.3.M12685 Ho 2002 [E]—dc21 2001001884

ISBN 0-8050-6352-8

First Edition—2002

The artist used pencil on watercolor paper to create the illustrations for this book.

Designed by Martha Rago

Printed in the United States of America on acid-free paper. ∞

5 7 9 10 8 6

Hondo & Fabian

written and illustrated by

Peter McCarty

Henry Holt and Company

New York

Fabian on the windowsill,

Hondo on the floor—

two sleepy pets

in their favorite places.

"Wake up, Hondo.

Time to go!"

Hondo will have an adventure.

Fabian will stay home.

Where is Hondo going,
riding in a car?

Hondo is going to the beach
to meet his friend Fred.

Fabian is going to
the living room
to play with the baby.

Two happy dogs

dive in the waves.

Fabian dives for the door.

Hondo has fun with Fred.

Fabian has fun too.

Now Hondo is getting hungry.

He wishes he could eat the fish.

Fabian is getting hungry too.
He wishes he could eat
the turkey sandwich.

At last Hondo comes home.

It's time for dinner!

Side by side Hondo and Fabian

eat their food.

Hondo and Fabian, full and fat—
in their favorite places once again.

"Good night, Hondo."
"Good night, Fabian."

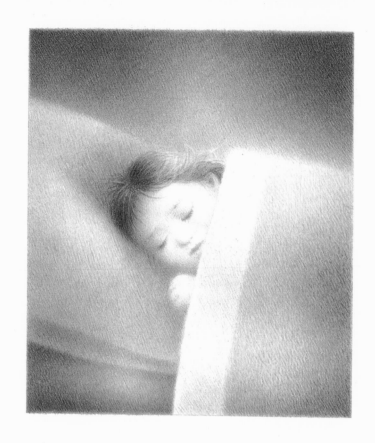

"Good night, baby!"

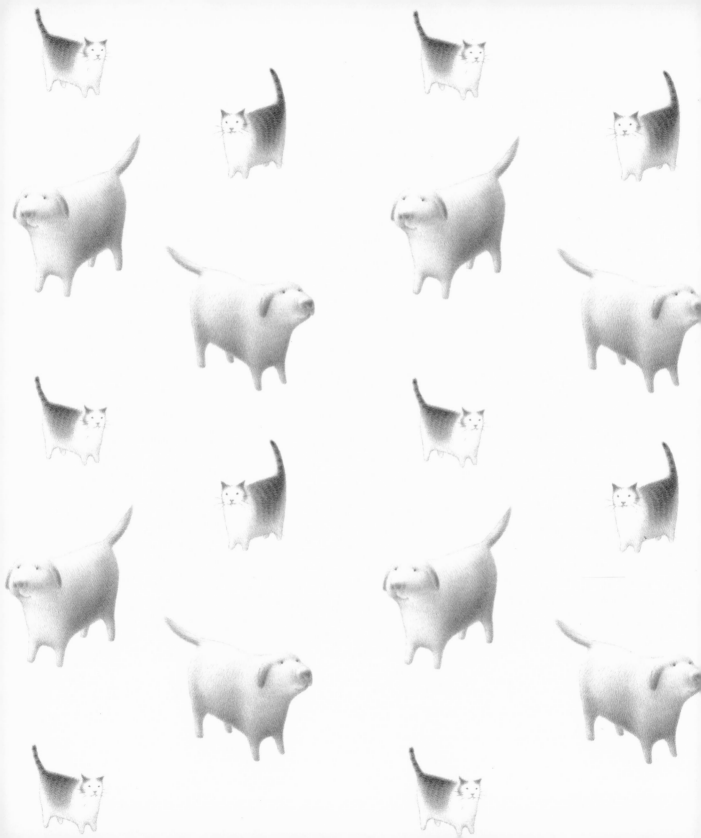